Groundhog's Runaway Shadow

David Biedrzycki

Charlesbridge

The only thing that could keep up with little Phil Groundhog was . . .

. . . his shadow!

No matter how fast he ran . . .

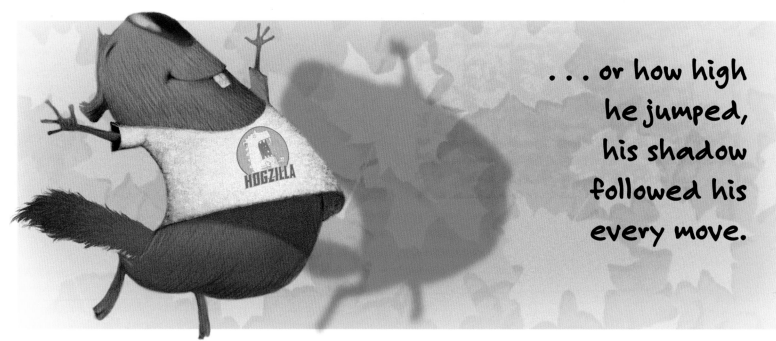

. . . or how high he jumped, his shadow followed his every move.

Whether he laughed . . .

. . . or cried,

his shadow was always right there beside him.

Even when Phil felt small . . .

. . . his shadow could make him feel bigger.

♫ Pretty hippos out walkin' with gorillas down my street! ♫

But everyone grows up.

Even groundhogs and their shadows.

Grown-up groundhogs
are expected to act
a certain way.

But Phil's shadow
had other plans.

Phil's idea of the perfect vacation was taking the bus to the local beach.

Shadow dreamed of visiting faraway places.

Phil loved scary movies.
Shadow, not so much.

Phil enjoyed eating dandelions, clover, and tree bark.

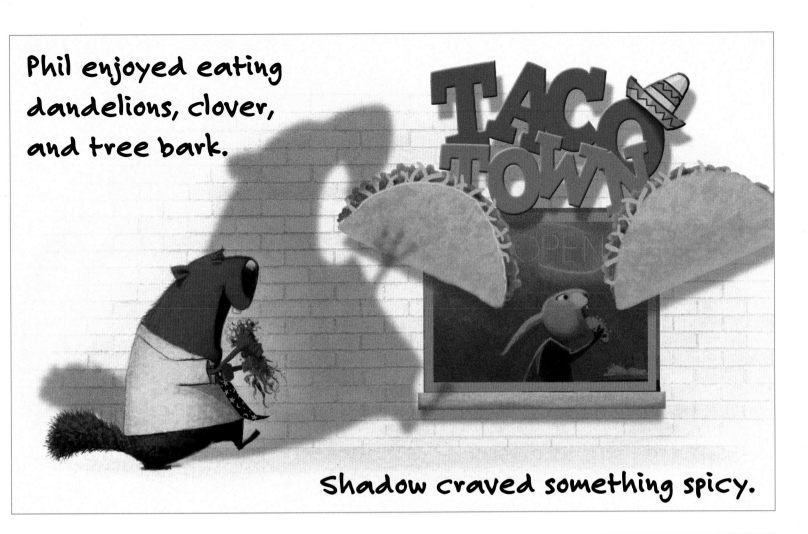

Shadow craved something spicy.

Phil liked to be on time.
Shadow liked to stop and smell the roses.

At first Phil found Shadow's behavior amusing . . .

. . . but a little off-key.

Phil's friends
found it amazing . . .

. . . and a little . . .

. . . gross.

But soon it got annoying . . .

. . . and then downright embarrassing.

Phil had had enough.

Why can't you be like other shadows?

I wish you would just go away!

Shadow was crushed.

He got angry.

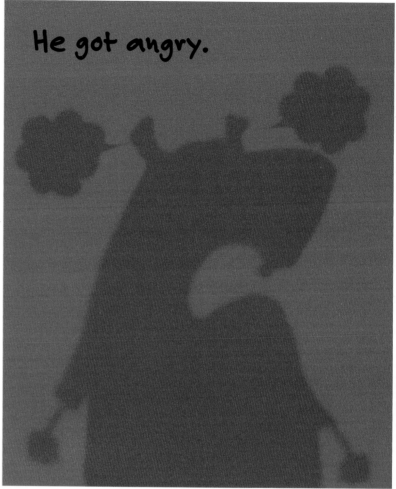

But then he thought about it.

Phil said he should go away.

And he had always wanted to travel.

So that night . . .

. . . and the
        next morning . . .

. . . and a couple
       of days later . . .

Back at home, Phil tried everything to find his shadow.

He posted signs.

LOST

HAVE YOU SEEN MY SHADOW?
IF FOUND,
KEEP SHADOW OUT OF
SHADE AND CALL

555-5555

IMMEDIATELY.

He used the newspaper.

Punxsutawney

GROUNDHOG
SEEKS
SHADOW

Fun-loving homebody groundhog is looking for lost shadow. Please come back, Shadow, so we can hibernate together. I promise things will be different.

DOG
SEEKS
BEST FRIE

Looking for adventurous explore the world. I enjoy walks on the beach, playing or cuddling by the fire in a mountain cabin. Present me treats and I'll be eating out o your hand for a lifetime. Contact Punxsutaw

SKUNK

Then he saw Shadow making news . . .

Punxsutawney Post

Mysterious Shadow Seen at Eiffel Tower

Halfway around the world, Shadow realized something was missing. He had no one to share in his adventures.

The thought of searching for Shadow scared Phil silly.

He'd have to travel far and wide.

But the next morning . . .

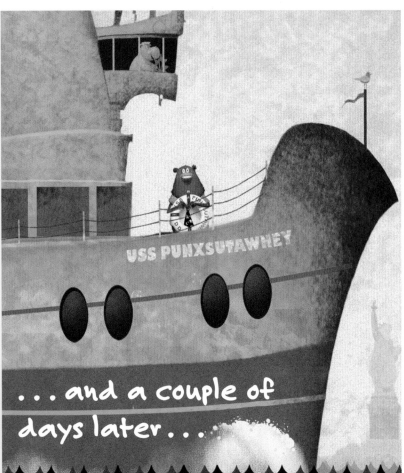

. . . and a couple of days later . . .

. . . and into the following week . . .

. . . that's exactly what he did.

He searched . . .

Shadow?

. . . and searched . . .

. . . and searched some more.

Finally, when he could search
no longer, he had an idea.

He began
to play.

And when he did . . .

. . . he heard someone . . .

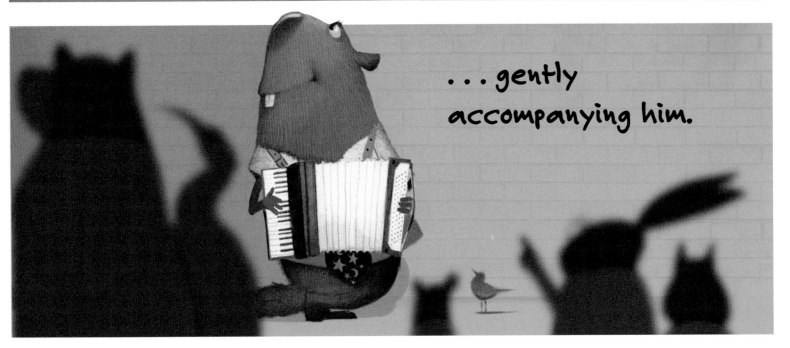

. . . gently accompanying him.

The two friends played together,
this time in perfect harmony.

And the next morning,
and a couple of
days later,
and forever after,
that's exactly
what they did.

(Except sometimes on February 2!)

Shadow?

Can you find the sixteen hidden Pennsylvanias in the book?

To Justin, Alec, and Julia, whose shadows never stray.
Special thanks to the amazing Nicholas Rivera.

Published by Charlesbridge
85 Main Street
Watertown, MA 02472
(617) 926-0329
www.charlesbridge.com

Illustrations done in Adobe Photoshop
Hand lettering by Julia Biedrzycki
Text type set in Felt Tip Bold by Mark Simonson
Color separations by Colourscan Print Co Pte Ltd, Singapore
Printed by 1010 Printing International Limited in Huizhou,
   Guangdong, China
Production supervision by Brian G. Walker
Designed by Diane M. Earley

Library of Congress Cataloging-in-Publication Data
Names: Biedrzycki, David, author, illustrator.
Title: Groundhog's Runaway Shadow / David Biedrzycki.
Description: Watertown, MA : Charlesbridge, [2016] | Summary: Little
   Phil Groundhog and his shadow do everything together, but when
   they grow up the more adventurous shadow wants to travel, so he
   leaves—but neither is happy, so Phil goes searching for his friend.
Identifiers: LCCN 2016013770 (print) | LCCN 2016015128 (ebook)
   | ISBN 9781580897341 (reinforced for library use)
   | ISBN 9781607348948 (ebook) | ISBN 9781607348955 (ebook pdf)
Subjects: LCSH: Woodchuck—Juvenile fiction. | Shades and
   shadows—Juvenile fiction. | Friendship—Juvenile fiction. | CYAC:
   Woodchuck—Fiction. | Shadows—Fiction. | Friendship—Fiction.
Classification: LCC PZ7.B4745 Gr 2016 (print) | LCC PZ7.B4745 (ebook)
   | DDC [E]—dc23
LC record available at https://lccn.loc.gov/2016013770

Printed in China
(hc) 10 9 8 7 6 5 4 3 2 1